Rosa's Diary

Written by Rita Benson

Illustrated by Caroline Campbell

Thursday, February 15th

Dear Diary,
Yesterday after school, Mama took me to the library downtown. I was really excited. I'd never been there before and I've already read all the really good books in our school library. When our family came here from Italy, we brought lots of books with us, but none of them are in English.

The librarian took me over to the children's book section and asked me what sort of book I wanted to read. I looked at the rows and rows of books and didn't know what to choose.

"Well," she said, "here's one you might like. It's an adventure about some children who travel to another planet."

I started the book right away, and I read all the way home in the car. I was on another planet, hearing strange noises and about to discover a mysterious creature...
and that was the moment we arrived home! I had to help Mama unload the car and set the table.

At bedtime, I was only halfway through the story when Mama came to kiss me goodnight and turn out the light. So, after she went back to the living room, I got up quietly and tiptoed past the door. I took the flashlight out of the kitchen drawer, crept back to bed and went on reading about the creatures trapped in the underground city.

This morning when I woke up, the book was on the floor and the flashlight batteries were dead.

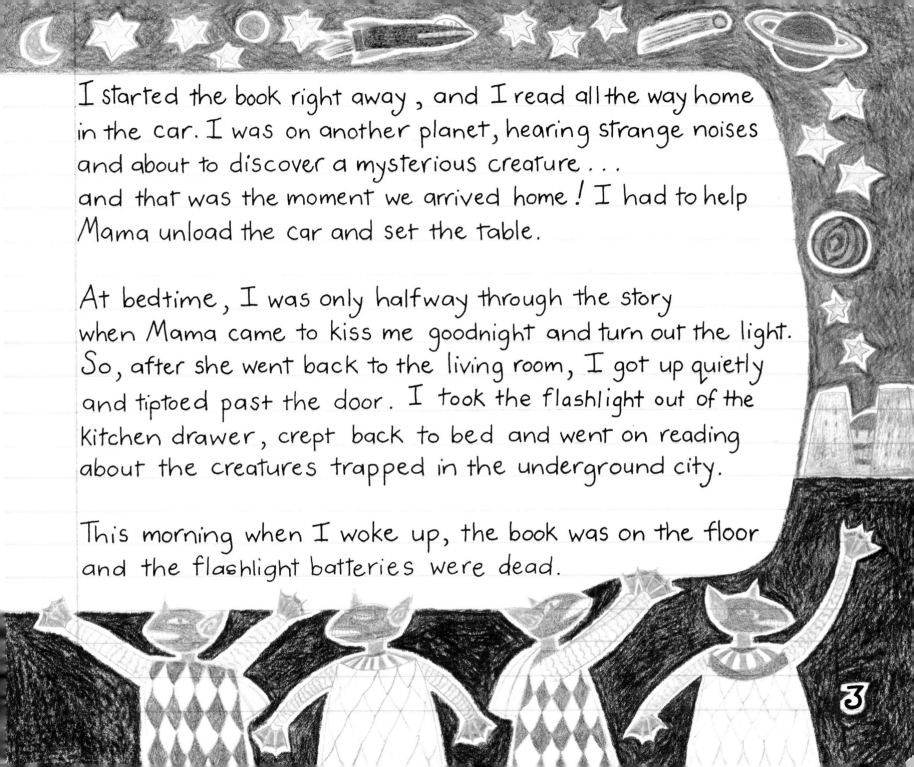

Friday, February 16th

Dear Diary,
I still haven't been able to finish my book. After school
we had people over - the people who have moved into the apartment
next to ours. When I got home, Alex (he's my little brother)
and I had to help in the kitchen, as well as clean our rooms
and the rest of the apartment.

We went to bed late and I couldn't find any new batteries
for the flashlight, so I still don't know if the children escaped
from the hairy creature.

I'm writing this in school again. Our teacher, Mr. Mills, is great.
He lets us write in our diaries if we have finished our other work.
When he first told us we had to write a diary, I thought
I wouldn't have anything to write about, but I was wrong.

Saturday, February 17th

Dear Diary,
I finished my book this morning! It was great!
I had to be really sneaky to get it finished though. Every Saturday
morning I help Mama clean the apartment. But this morning,
before Mama could call me to help her, I sneaked out to the
back shed where Papa stores his tools. I just **had** to find
out if the children got back to earth safely.

When Mama called me, I tried to read faster. I only had
a few pages to go. When I finished it I sat there in a daze.
I hardly knew where I was for a few minutes.
Then I rushed to find Mama. She was looking rather cross
from all the calling, but I asked if she'd drive me to the library
again, so I could get another book. She said we had to do our chores
now and that I'd have to wait till our next shopping day.
Well, I just **can't** wait!

5

Wednesday, February 21st

Dear Diary,

I haven't had time to write for a few days because
we've had a lot of homework. I don't really mind it because now
I'm starting to enjoy school. I can still remember my first year
at school when I was learning to speak English.
I used to sit at my desk and try to understand what the teacher
was saying. I knew quite a lot of English words but I didn't
use them very often. They sounded so strange when I practiced
them in bed at night.

6

I remember the day the teacher asked some of the children
to draw a picture on the board about what sort of day it was
outside. Then she held out the chalk to me and asked
if I would like to try it. I got out of my seat and took the chalk.
Through the window I could see the sun and the clouds
and the blue sky.

So I used white and blue and drew a square which was full
of clouds and sky. I added a few streaks of yellow for the sun.
When I sat down I heard giggling and I had a closer look at what
everyone else had drawn. Did I feel silly! Everyone else had
drawn pictures of people fishing and swimming and playing
in the park. The teacher said she liked my picture but I think
she was just being nice.

Thursday, February 22nd

Dear Diary,

Shopping day! Library day! Hooray!

Friday, February 23rd

Dear Diary,

Guess what? The book I got from the library yesterday is **really** boring. The cover looked OK but I should have read the paragraph on the back that tells you what it's about. Boxing! Can you believe it?

Sunday, February 25th

Dear Diary,

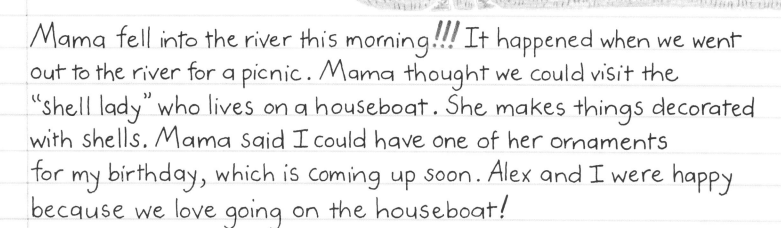

Mama fell into the river this morning!!! It happened when we went out to the river for a picnic. Mama thought we could visit the "shell lady" who lives on a houseboat. She makes things decorated with shells. Mama said I could have one of her ornaments for my birthday, which is coming up soon. Alex and I were happy because we love going on the houseboat!

Well, we were all looking for a spot to have our lunch, when Alex's hat fell down the river bank. Mama was scrambling down to get it when she slipped into the water. She tried to hold onto the tree branches that hung into the river, but they were very slimy and she kept slipping back into the water.

We screamed, and Papa jumped in after her, with all his clothes on, and dragged her out.

Alex and I hugged and hugged her—we were all so relieved!

Monday, February 26th

Dear Diary,

We have some baby rabbits! Papa has never let us have rabbits
before because he says they are pests. But yesterday
he brought home two, one for each of us.
Alex has called his rabbit Peter, because his teacher is reading
them a book about a rabbit who is called Peter. I called mine
Lucy.

12

Tuesday, February 27th

Dear Diary,

This morning, Peter and Lucy had eaten only some of the grass
and carrot we gave them last night. Papa told us not to worry.
He says we probably couldn't starve them if we tried!

13

Thursday, March 1st

Dear Diary,

We're going to the library after school today. At last!
I can take back that boring book.

Friday, March 2nd

Dear Diary,

I found a great book! You just won't believe it, but it's about a girl called Rosa (just like me), who came from Italy (just like me). **And** it's about the bad times she had when she first went to school.

She started off badly from the very first day. Her mother couldn't fill out the forms in English, so the teacher did it. Her mother told the teacher that she "had finished six last September," so the teacher put her down as being seven years old. But her mother really meant that she **turned** six in September!
That is just the way they say it in Italy. So Rosa was put in the wrong class, and it was very difficult for her.

Lucy seems a lot bigger already. I hope I'll be able to take her to school soon.

Sunday, March 4th

Dear Diary,

Yesterday, Mama was angry with me for reading my book while I was supposed to be setting the table. I really like this book, but it is very sad in places.

Sometimes the other kids tease Rosa, especially about her long hair. Every morning, before her mother goes to work, she spends a long time combing it into ringlets that reach right down Rosa's back.

When she goes to school, some of the children circle around her singing, "Ringlet-ringlet-Rosie," like in that rhyme. Sometimes they crowd around her and pull the ringlets. Her mother always asks her how her hair gets so messy and Rosa always lies and tells her that it's from playing on the swings. She doesn't want her mother to know that the other children tease her.

Wednesday, March 7th

Dear Diary,

Alex's rabbit escaped last night. It took us about an hour to find him!

Thursday, March 8th

Dear Diary,

I finished the book last night and I was really glad
it had a happy ending. Rosa made a friend. One day, in art class,
a girl called Janice asked if Rosa would like to sit with her
at lunch time. Rosa was so happy.

But when she was eating her lunch with Janice, she tried
to hide the thick slices of homemade bread and salami,
and the black olives. She really wished her mother
would give her peanut butter sandwiches, like everyone else.

Janice thought the olives were plums, and popped one in her mouth. She liked it, though, and took another one. Anyway, after that Rosa and Janice often ate their lunch together, and Rosa always brought extra olives for Janice.

Wasn't that terrific? I think Janice must have been a bit like my best friend, Clare.
(Except that Clare doesn't like olives.)

Me

Clare

Friday, March 9th

Dear Diary,

We didn't go downtown yesterday because the car wouldn't start. Alex and I got a message in class to catch the bus. When we got home, Papa said that Mama took the bus to do the shopping, and we could walk over to our grandparents' apartment.

Nonno Mimo was ready for us when we got there. We sat at the big kitchen table and he gave us lemonade and a slice of Nonna Maria's homemade bread with plenty of butter and ricotta cheese. Alex and I love the smell of fresh bread.

Sunday, March 11th

Dear Diary,

Nonna Maria let us help her bake bread yesterday.
Alex and I helped measure the flour and salt and yeast
into the bowls. Then we stirred and squished and kneaded
the dough until it was ready for the oven. When the first batch
of bread was done baking, Nonna Maria took out two small loaves,
buttered them and gave us one each.
I **love** Nonna's bread! She sent us home with a big bag
full of warm loaves.

21

Monday, March 12th

Dear Diary,

It's my birthday on Thursday and we are going to have a party.
All my uncles and aunts and cousins are coming,
as well as Nonno and Nonna. Mama says we have
to clean the apartment so that everything will look nice.

Mama said that Nonna Maria has got something really special
for me this year, something from the old country. I wonder
what it could be.
Only three more days till my birthday!

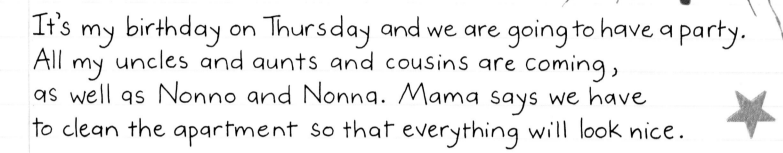

Wednesday, March 14th

Dear Diary,

23

Friday, March 16th

Dear Diary,

I had the best birthday ever! Nonna Maria gave me a white linen bedspread made of flax. It's really old. Years ago, when Nonna was young, she and her own mother made it on a hand loom. She said that after they had soaked the flax plants in water for a few days, they threshed out all the fibers, and wove them into cloth. Then Nonna spent months and months embroidering the cloth and making the wide lace border. I will treasure it always.

I got lots of other presents, too, but best of all I got a beautiful shell jewelry box. And do you know what else? Mama found out from the librarian that there is a sequel to that book about Rosa and she has ordered it for me at the bookstore!

This was the best birthday I ever had!